The Clearing in the Wood

To JAMIE SEABOLT
THANK YOU
FOR TEACHING
MY SON ABOUT SCIENCE
WITH BEST WISHES

The Clearing in the Wood

Warren C. Edick II

This is a work of fiction. Names, characters, places
and incidents either are the product of the author's
imagination or are used fictitiously, and any resemblance
to any actual persons, living or dead, events, or locales is
entirely coincidental.

This book was printed in the United States of America.

Cover pictures by Susanne Edick.
www.theclearinginthewood.com

To order additional copies of this book, contact:
Xlibris Corporation
1-888-795-4274
www.Xlibris.com
Orders@Xlibris.com
82843

duhkhaanta, tragoedia, tragedy

It was a rainy day. The sky was dark and roared with occasional thunder as the procession slowly made its way toward the hilltop. The bearers of the casket slowed to baby steps to ensure their footing on the wet ground. Baby steps, yes, I remember well. When Adam and I met, we talked about babies all the time. We were both fond of children and were easily led to believe that our parenting skills would be naturally superior. It was a time full of promise.

The rain started picking up and umbrellas popped open. Most umbrellas were black just like the attire of the day. The grass to each side of the procession was soggy and at times even muddy such that all filed in rank to remain on the path. No one spoke. I felt strangely uncomfortable throughout not knowing what was expected of me. Was I to invite the funeral party to a gathering thereafter? I did not dislike them. I simply was not capable.

Adam and I met in college when he was a graduate student. I was an undergraduate. Entering college was a liberating experience for me. It was a time when I had just severed myself from the mold of my upbringing. I had been raised catholic and had graduated from a Jesuit High School. During this time

Fr. Bob, one of the Jesuit priests appointed to our care, had introduced me to the ways of science. I remember him telling me during a confessional that to some extent, at least, we were called to believe in evolution. I thought him most reasonable. More and more I found myself drawn toward science at the expense of my faith. And finally, entering college, I declared my major in physics with a minor in comparative religions. The minor was intended to appease my parents should they disapprove of my major in physics. Surprisingly they did not. Instead, they supported my decision.

Entering college as an aspiring physicist I became immersed in the Big Bang theory and thermodynamics along with Darwin, Einstein, Hawkins, and so on. I stopped going to church. I had come face-to-face with my personal renaissance and my very own age of enlightenment. And then I met Adam. Adam was a handsome young man. He was six feet tall, slender with blond hair, and deep blue eyes. Among his professors he had established himself as a favorite. He had earned a teaching assistantship that allowed him to grade freshmen courses in his field, which was biology. A freshman myself, I looked up to him as I would the following twenty-four years. Adam had always been pleased with my understanding of Charles Darwin, and I had always been impressed with his commitment to the Big Bang theory when thinking about the origin of the world.

We graduated the same year. He earned his doctorate in biology, and I my bachelors in physics with the minor in comparative religions. We had little free time during my junior and senior year. Earning my degree in physics proved tremendously laborious and Adam was consumed by his dissertation. During this time, though, we decided to get married after school and have children. It is therefore that I made the decision to commit to Adam and our future family instead of going to graduate school myself. We agreed that I could be a full time mom and become a part time substitute high school science teacher. This way I could stay active in my scientific aspirations as well as becoming a mother. Adam, on the other hand, landed a tenure track teaching position with a prestigious university along the Front Range of the Rocky Mountains. And so there we went expecting a picket fence, a golden retriever, and everything else.

Several years into our marriage we decided to subject ourselves to medical testing to figure out why I was seemingly unable to become pregnant. As it turned out, Adam was sterile and unable to cause me to conceive. At this time Adam's career demanded much attention precluding me from returning to school myself. Adam suggested we adopt a child as soon as his work allowed, but this suggestion never came to pass. And so I, more or less, became a professional substitute science teacher and rationalized my life by my commitment to our marriage, while in truth Adam procured a healthy income allowing me to live a life of great comfort and little challenge.

By now it was pouring. The priest presiding over Adam's funeral was unhurried nonetheless. Others, however, were getting impatient. I myself could care a less. Here I stood, forty-two years old, no makeup, no children, no husband, and no career. My parents had passed along some years back and I was alone. Adam fell ill three years ago and was diagnosed with terminal brain cancer. His condition deteriorated rapidly. I gave care to him as long as I could. Yet he, nevertheless, spent the last six months in a hospice where he was unresponsive and no longer mentally present.

Overwhelmed by medical expenses and emotional drain it seemed nothing but fitting for it to be a dreary day. And so it happened that the bearers of the casket slowly lowered Adam into the earth. All along, a colleague of Adam had held an umbrella over me but I had not noticed. Not until the priest offered me a small shovel and indicated that I move some earth into the grave. I gripped the small shovel firmly, sank it into the wet soil, and released the earth onto the casket. Curiously, it sounded almost hollow as the soil struck it from above. Slowly I turned around and gave back the shovel to the priest as I noticed a small pin attached to his lapel that carried the letters "S" and "J" within it. It stood for Societe Jesuit. The priest was a Jesuit.

Leaving the funeral I told Adam's colleagues that I wished to be alone when they offered me their comfort. Walking away, I desired not to be comforted at all because to my own surprise I did not feel sad in the least. Instead, what I felt was anger. I had been lied to—now I was angry. I was angry with myself, angry with Adam, angry with my parents, angry at my life, and angry at science. I was supposed to have children and raise them free of foolish superstitions, a respected husband who was an active member of the scientific community, a calling that allowed me to engage high school students and tell them about the true beginning of the world, and much more.

I stopped and turned around. On top of the hill two gravediggers finished the job. I walked back up to the grave and stood next to the workers as they filled it shovel by shovel.

Drenching wet and shivering I recalled the heartbreaking events of the recent past.

Wishing to calm my mind during Adam's stay in the hospice I had visited some physics symposiums on the Big Bang theory. The first one I attended was very technical and much to my liking. Yet there he appeared for the first time, a young man, perhaps in his early twenties. Toward the end of the presentations he raised his hand and asked the following question with a politeness that was impeccable:

"Dear sirs, what was before the Big Bang?"

Several graduate students in the rear of the stage chuckled and even laughed at the question. The presenting professor glanced back at them to affirm their sentiments and thereby forewarned the audience that those on stage knew something others did not.

"Well, young man," the professor continued, "it needs to be understood that with the Big Bang there came into existence not only matter but time and space itself. It is thus that there was no time *before* the Big Bang. Therefore, there cannot be such a thing as *before* the Big Bang because the word *before* is a temporal indicator. In short, the meaning of the word *before* exists only within time and not outside of it. And since time did not exist until the Big Bang, it follows that the question as to what was *before* the Big Bang does not exist."

How eloquently said, I thought as I identified myself with the row of gleaming graduate students to the rear of the stage.

17

Little did I know at the time that this polite young man would end up undoing the entire world I cherished and believed in.

vidyāa, philosophia, philosophy

It was two months later at another physics symposium, this time on thermodynamics and the Big Bang theory. The same young man appeared in the audience and sat one row in front of me. The presentations of several award-winning physicists ended in a standing ovation, as the crowd seemed awestruck before such grandiose a science. As calm reentered the room, the young man raised his hand and most humbly asked the following question:

"Dear sirs, what *caused* the Big Bang?"

This time the professors on stage glanced at each other as if determining who should answer this question when one of them rose, seemingly with the approval of the others, and began speaking:

"The question thus put demands an analysis into the theory of causation."

The professor let out a slight cough so as to clear his throat.

"You see," he calmly continued, "causation is a way of determining the transference of energy in general, and perhaps of kinetic energy in particular. More simply to put, it is a way of describing motion. That is to say, matter as it is found on the periodic table of elements does not move if it is not moved upon. Just think of an event "A" that brings about another event, that is, event

"B." Here we say that the first event "A" is the *cause* of the second event "B," and the second event "B" is then the *effect* of the first event "A."

Here again the professor cleared his throat and quickly turned to capture the approval of the others before continuing.

"In science, we view each entity or event as an observable entity or event such that we see two entities or events. Namely, the first event "A" followed by the second event "B." Hence, in causal theory we speak of the *antecedent* event, which is the cause, and the *consequent* event, which is the effect. Please note that *antecedent* event here refers to that event which occurs *prior* or *before* the second event. Likewise, a *consequent* event refers to that event which takes place *after* the event that preceded it."

"What follows from this is that a causal event happens *before* that event which is called its effect such that when one asks for the cause of the Big Bang, one is actually asking for what came *before* the Big Bang. Yet, there was no *before* the Big Bang because time itself came into being only with the Big Bang. And therefore one can see that the question as to what caused the Big Bang really does not exist."

The professor paused, captured the approval of the others on the stage behind him and then turned and motioned to the audience to elicit their approval as well. I myself exaggerated the movement of my head up and down, as did many others, when the young man elegantly raised his hand again and asked the following question:

"What about *cotemporaneous* causation?"

The on-stage professor looked bewildered and asked the young man to explain himself. The young man continued:

"Dear professors, are we to believe that you have never heard of *cotemporaneous* causation? It is that part of causal theory that must contend with two events happening simultaneously, or, at the same time. Yet, nonetheless, it is readily ascertainable which one of the two events is the *cause* and which one is the *effect*. Please allow me to demonstrate."

The young man left his seat and approached a whiteboard that was situated in the aisle just in front of the stage. Reaching for a marker he demonstrated the following. He held the marker tightly in his hand as he set its felt-tip on the board. Then, after a short pause, he moved the marker up and down on the whiteboard and thereby drew a wavelength shaped figure. Releasing the marker he turned to the professors and asked:

"Which moved first, the marker or my hand?"

Now addressing the audience he continued:

"Clearly the marker started moving at the exact moment my hand started moving that was holding it. Both events, then, the marker moving and my hand moving, happened simultaneously, which is to say, at the same time. Nevertheless, is there anyone here who believes that it cannot be established which event *caused* the other? Likewise, is there anyone here who believes that the marker moving *caused* my hand to move? Or is it plain that my hand moving in fact *caused* the marker to move?"

Once again turning to the whiteboard, the young man drew a crude but effective picture of a steam locomotive with two boxcars and a caboose attached to it.

Then, addressing the audience, he calmly continued, "Let's use the late Prof. Taylor's example and say we inch the locomotive forward and thereby remove any and all slack that may be present in the couplings connecting the cars. And then we come to a complete stop! Now we tell the engineer to move the locomotive forward again only one inch. Given, however, that there is no slack in the couplings, it follows that the boxcars and the caboose move forward by exactly one inch as well. Furthermore, though, because there was no slack in the couplings at all, it also follows that the caboose, for example, moved forward one inch at the exact same moment the locomotive moved forward by one inch."

"Thus, both the caboose and the locomotive moved at exactly the same time. Nevertheless, is there anyone here who wishes to claim that the caboose *caused* the locomotive to move? Likewise, is there anyone here who wishes to claim that it is impossible to decide which of the two *caused* the other to move, the caboose or the locomotive? Clearly, we can all discern that it was in fact the locomotive that *caused* the caboose to move."

"And since both events happened at the same time, there can be no talk as to an *antecedent* or *prior* event causing a *consequent* one. Both the locomotive and the caboose started moving at the very same moment. To be sure, though, one event did in fact *cause* the other, namely, the locomotive moving *caused* the caboose to move. Yet, these events occurred simultaneously."

"And it is therefore," the young man now addressing everyone in the room, "that the question as to the *cause* of the Big Bang cannot be simply reduced to temporal language and be met with the claim that time itself came into being with the Big Bang, because the *cause* of the Big Bang **could** have happened at the same moment of, rather than *before,* the Big Bang. And albeit true that time and space came into being with the Big Bang, should there have been a Big Bang, and also true that there is overwhelming evidence in favor of the Big Bang theory, the question still exists and is very real: Dear sirs, what *caused* the Big Bang?"

The presenting professor seemed unsure as he turned to his colleagues in want of a response. His colleagues, in turn, raised their eyebrows so as to be stumped when the oldest of them, who sat off to the side, slowly rose from his chair and made his way to the front of the stage. And speaking into the microphone he calmly said:

"Young man, we physicists, as a field, can say nothing about that!"

"Thank you, sir" the young man replied politely and got up, made his way to the aisle, and left the room. The other professors were still whispering to each other in what appeared to be an effort to bridge an awkward moment whereas the old man slowly returned to his seat and sat down just as content as one could possibly be.

The audience had grown silent.

"Lady," the man said, "lady, you're going to catch a pneumonia. Please join us in the chapel."

I looked around and saw that the gravediggers had put aside their shovels and were heading for shelter. The rain was pouring down fiercely. Soaking wet I signaled them I would remain. He joined his colleague on the way to the chapel. Looking down I saw that

Adam's grave had been almost filled in. The sky roared and bellowed. I looked up and noticed a peculiar darkness in the middle of the day.

That day at the physics symposium my world had been turned upside down. How was this possible that the Big Bang could have been caused my something other than itself? More than twenty years I had held fast to the belief that the Big Bang was the *ultimate* beginning of the world. There was nothing else outside of it. It explained everything and thereby excluded all the childish thought of miracles and the like. Why would the most senior of the professors allow for such a reversal in ideas? And worse yet, how was it possible that such a simple exchange of words could threaten my entire worldview and thereby just about everything I believed in?

Adam, at the time of this physics presentation, had already been vegetative and lie dying in the hospice. I, on the other hand, was furious as piece by piece my life became subject to annihilation.

The rain let up a little and I noticed my shoes were caked in mud. Just then I heard a bird, somewhat distant, but nevertheless, a singing bird.

A week after the symposium I headed to the Colorado State University where I had made an appointment with the old physicist. To my surprise he had returned my phone call and offered to meet with me. Arriving at his office I found the door wide open.

"Come on in," he spoke invitingly upon seeing my head pop into the room.

After brief introductions I summed up my concerns to him, all along making sure I expressed my displeasure as well.

Toward the end of my whining he gracefully interrupted me by saying:

"Do you know who the young man was who kept us all honest that day?"

"No," I replied.

"He was a philosopher," the old man continued. "You see, philosophy is the very source of science, properly speaking."

"And he was right! Although a good theory, the question of the *ultimate* origin of the world is not at all settled by the Big Bang."

Eyes wide open I exclaimed, "But what could have possibly caused the Big Bang?"

"Well," the old man went on patiently, "either it all came out of nothing or something has always existed."

"Out of nothing?" I uttered skeptically. "But that is not possible. That would be an *uncaused* event, which would violate the law of causation. Nothing can come from nothing!"

"That's exactly what it would be, an *uncaused* event," he added. "By the way, an *uncaused* event is what others may simply call a *miracle*. How do you feel about that?"

"Sir, with all due respect, I did not come here to discuss *miracles.*"

"Oh, but you have milady! You see, if we reject the possibility that it all came from nothing, then we must consider that *something* has always existed. And this something can only be one of two things. Either the world has always existed, that is to say, we are dealing with an infinite regression of causes into an infinite past, or the world came about supernaturally, which is to say, a God caused it, who is her or himself *uncaused*. The old Greeks referred to this as an *unmoved mover.*"

"The interesting thing to note, however, is that these three possibilities completely exhaust the issue. It all either came from nothing, or has always existed, or was brought into being supernaturally, that is to say, by a supernatural force we may refer to as God. In other words, there will *never* be another option. Try as you will, invent any story you fancy concerning the *ultimate* beginning of

33

the world, any whatsoever and it will always reduce into one of these three possibilities!"

The professor paused and leaned back into his chair.

Speaking softly and much slower than before he gently added, "And you see, if the world has always existed, in one form or another, then it has been *caused* to exist by nothing. Because if it has always been, then nothing has ever brought it about. This, then, is also an *uncaused* event, for nothing *caused* it to be if it has *always* been. So regardless of whether or not it all came from nothing, or whether or not it has always existed, we are looking at an *uncaused* event. And if a God created it all, well, then we are looking at a *supernatural* event. Therefore, we have to consider *uncaused* events or a *supernatural* event, because all three options, in the end, are *miraculous.*"

A silence filled the room as I stared at the professor and he looked back at me.

Finally he continued, "What is noteworthy here is that all three possibilities lead into some form of deism, that is to say, the belief in a god, for if the world is *uncaused,* as in the case of it having existed eternally, and in addition, it is able to become aware of itself, which in fact it is given that you and I are here, for example, it follows that the world itself is a god. This form of belief is called *pantheism,* where *pan* is the ancient Greek word for *nature.* And since *nature* so conceived possesses a *miraculous* being in addition to manifesting awareness, it follows that existence as a whole, namely, *nature itself*, is a god."

"And the same holds true if the world came to be out of nothingness. Here too its existence is *miraculous* for being *uncaused,* in addition to it manifesting self-awareness in at least the form of us being here. Both of these options, then, demand a belief in *pantheism* where nature itself must be seen as a deity."

"Moreover, though, there is the third possibility of a *supernatural* God having miraculously created the entire thing, which is the position of many religions in the world. And these are all the possibilities there will ever be as these three possibilities are logically exhaustive, and, therefore, preclude any further options. Strictly speaking, then, both *atheism* and *agnosticism* are unwarranted positions, for they are logically untenable. Whereas atheism denies any god whatsoever, be it a natural one or otherwise, agnosticism suspends judgment while waiting on another possibility that will never come."

"But I don't understand," I stuttered in bewilderment. "How can this be? Why does no one know about this?"

"But some of us do," he answered calmly. "Albert Einstein, for example, immediately discarded the *atheism* of his youth once he understood this very analysis. He chose to believe in the option where the world has always existed and therefore embraced the idea of *pantheism,* the position that existence as a whole, that is to say, *nature* itself, is a god."

"You must know, my dear, that there is much false pride in science. Many foolishly cling to the idea that science has to do only with what is observable such that if you cannot see it, measure it, and weigh it, it is not considered science. What you need to know, though, is that numbers, for example, cannot be observed or weighed either. All we can represent in physical space are symbols of numbers that we write down. Nonetheless, it is naive to think that anyone could have ever skipped and danced on the moon without mathematics. Science, therefore, is not just seeing, but rather, *seeing* **AND** *thinking.*"

Once again leaning back into his chair he let out a sigh and remarked, "The best kept secret of the last two generations of Western civilization is that the Big Bang theory does not explain anything concerning the *ultimate* origin of the world. Yet many physicists will go through great lengths to hide this truth . . ."

"Yes," I interrupted in astonishment. "The professor at the symposium . . . did he not already know of cotemporaneous or simultaneous *causation* as the young man was careful to point out?"

"He most certainly did," the old man replied.

"Does it then not follow," I continued "that his entire motivation to reduce the young man's question down to temporal language, so as to counter the argument, was deceitful and not at all in the service of truth?"

"Yes, milady, that is exactly what follows!"

Shivering uncontrollably I stood in the mud in front of Adam's grave. All seemed lost—my husband, my career in physics, our income, motherhood, a faith sacrificed to science, and now science itself was proving inadequate as a substitute for any of them.

Life, which brimmed with promise, now felt as empty as I myself did. Nothing seemed as it did only months before. All appears to have been a lie, a profound betrayal. I had been a modern person. One who had figured it all out. Free of superstitions and the yoke of faith, free of guilt and anger, I was enlightened, illuminated, progressive, and tolerant! Liberated and intelligent were the operative words in my life. Yet here I stood, disillusioned, angry, and alone. It was a lie—every bit of it.

Arriving at home at last I was glad to be greeted by my dog Luna. It felt so good to have her jump up on me and wag her tail. Her unconditional joy echoed in the vast emptiness of what has become my being. And finally, laying down to rest, I fell unconscious for the night.

karuṇaa, grātia, friendship

The next morning there were bills that needed to be paid and I did not know how. I made a pot of coffee. My substitute teaching at the high school couldn't afford me the life I knew. I have to sell the house. I sipped the coffee. Adam's illness came unexpectedly. We had no children. The life insurance only covered his final expenses. I was running out of options, and for the first time in my life I simply did not know what to do.

There was a knock on the door. I put the cup on the counter. Strangely, though, Luna perked right up but remained silent instead of barking in her usual way. I opened the door to a crack to see who was there. It was the Jesuit priest from Adam's funeral.

"Hello, ma'am," he spoke slowly and in a very calm voice.

"Hello," I responded, surprised to see him.

"Forgive the intrusion," he continued, "but I wish to visit with you. May I come in?"

I hesitated for a moment but then opened the door wide.

"Yes, of course."

Showing the gentleman to the kitchen area I offered him coffee.

"How are you?" he asked cordially.

Immediately overcome by grief I lowered my head trying to hide the tears.

"I lost everything," I spoke. Regaining some composure I added, "How are you doing?"

"I am doing well now, but it hasn't always been that way," he responded. "Your husband was a biologist, was he not?"

"Yes, we both had committed our lives to science. My training is in physics."

"Ah, yes, physics. That is my field as well," he announced enthusiastically. "My Ph.D. is in physics," he added visibly excited.

"You have a doctorate in physics?"

"Yes, in nuclear physics. Though, most of my work revolved around theoretical physics. In fact, I'm a Big Bang theorist!"

"But how can that be?" I stuttered while raising my voice.

After a short moment of repose the priest softly continued, "Forgive me. My name is John. I am Fr. John. What is your name?"

"I am Vera," I now said calmly sipping my coffee.

"Well, Vera," the priest continued, "the physical world is very orderly and demands to be described, does it not?"

"Yes, I agree. But it leaves little room for souls and such," I answered timidly, trying to be sensitive toward the man's position in life.

"Well," speaking thoughtfully now, "I'm not sure that is the case. For example, when you opened the door for me and led me in, could you not have decided to tell me to come back later and shut the door?"

"Yes, of course."

"So you believe that you were free to do one or the other?"

"Yes. Obviously I could have decided either way . . ."

He interrupted me, "So you believe that holding the doorknob in your hand you could have freely decided to either close or open the door?"

"Yes!" I responded impatiently.

"Well then," he continued, "when your hand pulled on the knob in order to open the door, what was the immediate physical *cause* of that event? Was it not your hand and lower arm moving backwards and thereby opening the door instead of your hand and lower arm moving forward and thereby closing the door?"

"Yes, surely that was the reason why the door opened."

"And what was the physical *cause* of your hand and lower arm moving in that particular direction? Was it not due to muscles contracting in your upper arm that made your lower arm move in such a way?"

"Yes," I answered.

"The next question, then, physically speaking, is what made that muscle in your upper arm contract? Was it not a nerve leading from your spine to that muscle that was excited by electrochemical impulses that made the muscle contract?"

"Yes, it surely was," I concurred.

"Well, then what stimulated that particular nerve to do so? Was it not an electrochemical impulse from a different nerve leading from your brain down the spine to that nerve that *caused* it to fire? And what then *caused* the nerve leading out of your brain to fire? Was it not yet another nerve inside your brain that fired upon it?"

"Yes, clearly that was the case, but what does any of this have to do with souls?" I asked curiously.

Seemingly ignoring my question he continued, "Well, then what made that nerve inside your brain become excited so as to fire upon the one that followed? Clearly you would not have me believe that this nerve just started firing randomly or for no reason at all. This would be an *uncaused* event, or, in other words, a *miracle*. Therefore, physically speaking, it fired because it in turn was fired upon by yet another nerve that *caused* it to do so. And if we continue this journey backwards we will be following these physical *causes* from one physical event to the one before it, all the way back to the day you were born! Each physical event starting from your hand and lower arm moving to open the door, the muscle contracting in your upper arm, all the way to individual nerves being *caused* to fire by others firing upon them could be seen as individual domino pieces that fall on each other in a necessarily unbroken chain of succession. Is this not the case?"

"Physically speaking, this must be the case," I answered.

"Then how do you suppose yourself to be free?"

A moment of stillness engulfed us as I pondered the question. Puzzled, as if grasping for something elusive, I asked, "What do you mean?"

"Well," he continued, "it would appear that you were determined to open the door at that moment from the very day you were born. In fact, following this causal chain backwards further still, it would appear that you were determined to be born and open the door at that moment from the Big Bang on! In other words, if each domino fell exactly because it was fallen upon by the one before it, then you

49

actually had no say, whatever about opening the door for me."

The Jesuit smiled emitting a profound kindness.

Staring back at him agape my brain sparked.

"You see, if you were actually free, that is to say, if it was *ultimately* up to you whether or not you opened or closed the door on me at that moment, then there must have existed two different *causal* chains or rows of dominos. The one having resulted in your hand moving backwards so as to open the door, and the other having resulted in your hand moving forward so as to close it. Each of these two rows of dominos must therefore have a beginning, that is to say, a first domino or nerve that moves the subsequent

50

ones and thereby affects the outcome of whether or not the door opens or closes. And if you are truly free, then it is up to you which one of these two chains of events begins unfolding, the one resulting in you opening the door and the other in you closing it. But there cannot be a physical cause, that is to say, another domino before the first one that *causes* it to fall, for in this case there then is no beginning to the chain of physical events, no first domino, and we are back to having eliminated the possibility of freedom. For this chain of events would necessarily reach back to **before** you made your decision to open or close the door. Therefore, the first domino in either sequence will fall subsequent to your decision to open or close the door, but without some other domino or nerve having fallen or fired upon it. The challenge, of course, is that from a physical perspective alone this circumstance cannot be explained, for there simply is nothing on the periodic table of elements that can move without first having been moved upon!"

"But then what made the first domino fall?" I thought out loud. "Physically speaking, there then cannot have been a reason for it to fall. It would have just fallen as if moved by a ghost," I conceded sternly.

"Oh no, my dear," father uttered paternally, "we do not believe in ghosts. We call that the human soul!"

The priest left me that morning asking for permission to visit again the following day, a request I happily granted. That afternoon Luna and I went to the park. Luna would run all around smelling everything as if reading a book. Had an animal as much as brushed their fur against a twig, Luna would target the exact spot with her nose and was seemingly able to retrieve an unspoken amount of information about the animal that had gone before. Though, she also liked to play and cheer me up in any way she could. And so it came that we spent all of what was left of daylight just enjoying each other's company by running about on the grass.

The next morning I awoke early. Once again looking at the stack of bills, I decided to ignore them one last time and to prepare for the arrival of my new friend, Fr. John. I made coffee and set the table for two, just in case father would like some toast as well. And no sooner was I done than I heard him knocking on the door. I opened and showed him in. We sat down and he began talking.

"Well, Vera, how are you this morning?"

"I am doing well, Father, thank you," I replied.

"Were you able to reflect on the thoughts we shared?"

"Yes, I was. Last evening I thought about our conversation on human freedom. It seems to me that I have taken my freedom for granted without having given it much thought. In other words, I always thought I was free and that my mind is nothing other than my brain. It seems I never saw the contradiction inherent in the belief in freedom, on the one hand, and the belief that everything happens because of a physical reason, on the other. I am surprised of never having heard of such essential an idea."

"Ah, yes, it is the mind we are speaking of," he calmly answered.

"If, however, it is none other than an aspect of your brain, as modern physics would have us believe," he continued while sipping his coffee, "then it is essentially nothing other than matter, that is to say, a physical thing. In this way of thinking, in this model as it were, there is no room whatever for intentional freedom. In short, from this perspective there simply cannot be any events that are not *caused* by other physical events. Here, all is physical and your experience of freedom is therefore but an illusion, at best, or an outright grand hallucination. And although this attitude toward human freedom is presently taught in the lecture halls of physics around the world, it is usually kept under lock and key when physicists address the general public. Sadly, the reasons for this are rather sinister."

"What do you suppose those reasons are?" I inquired.

"Well, modern physics enjoys great reverence from the general public because of its profound successes. And rightly so, for landing on the moon is no small matter. Yet when denouncing human freedom publicly, many people rethink their respect for the physical sciences as it clearly removes human beings from moral responsibility for their actions. If free will is an illusion and we are determined to act in the ways we do, then we could not in fact have acted in any other way than we did. All of our actions are thus determined by *causal* circumstances over which we can have no control. How then could we be said to be responsible for these actions whatever they may be? Therefore, the denial of human freedom is rarely spoken of openly because it is unpopular. Moreover, most physicists live normal lives when they leave their laboratories at night, which generally demands them to believe in their own free will much as we believe in ours. In fact, we must assume ourselves free in order to deliberate and make but simple daily decisions. Essentially, avoiding the subject is a subtle form of deception. For denying free will is the very cornerstone of the dogma that those who wish to explore it are unreasonable, and, therefore, are not concerning themselves with what is real. This allows the physical sciences to perpetuate the idea that they have a monopoly on what is ultimately to be considered real. And according to this dogma, then, moral and human *values,* for example, are not considered real. I believe this to be a disservice toward the open and fair search for truth because considering free will, as we have done, strikes me as very reasonable."

"My mind, then, is what you consider to be my soul?"

"Yes, indeed. I personally have come to believe that the human mind cannot be reduced to a physical thing. Thus, when the body dies, which is a physical event, the mind may very well be able to continue on. It is therefore that I refer to it as your soul."

"But it cannot be proven to exist by observation. Is this not so?"

"No, it cannot! But it cannot be disproved either for observation in the scientific sense implies the use of our five senses. And since our five senses are physical organs that belong to our physical bodies, the only things they can observe are physical things. Thus, the widely held argument that a soul must be proven to exist by the physical sciences before it can be considered real, hinges on the idea that the soul which is by definition a non-physical thing must be observed by physical means that can only ever observe that which is physical in nature. In short, the argument itself is based on a grave contradiction rendering it utterly unreasonable and therefore also unscientific! The argument stacks the deck, so to speak,

59

and thereby embodies yet another deception. And deception, mind you, is a lie, which, of course, is the opposite of searching for truth."

At this point I found myself strangely relaxed. A curious peacefulness had overcome our conversation. Yet, becoming aware of it, restlessness began to return.

"How do you suppose to search for truth and keep deception at bay? Is such a thing possible?"

"Yes, I believe it is. Observation is seeing and we should strive to gain all the knowledge we can through seeing. The physical sciences are great tools to this end. But we must learn to follow our seeing with thinking. This is not always easy and nor is it always comfortable.

I learned of this many years ago on a journey I took into the wood. Please, allow me . . ."

Slowly raising from his chair the Jesuit signaled me to join him as we made our way to the living room window. Peering out the window he pointed to the mountains just west of town.

"There, do you see that mountain off in the distance?"

"Yes," I answered.

"Its name is *Mount Salubris*. Few people ever ascend it for it requires an overnight stay and is further away than one might be led to believe. To reach its peak one must traverse the wood, which stretches on and up for miles. A long time ago I undertook the journey. I was alone and in need of getting away. It was there that I learned of *seeing* **AND** *thinking*. It is a peculiar mountain. Yes, peculiar indeed . . ." he said as his voice gave way to silence.

"Well," suddenly shifting his attention, "it would seem that I must be on my way. Thank you for your time and for speaking with me. May I visit you again, Vera? It would mean much to me."

"Yes, Fr. John, please do," I answered. "Your company is most welcome."

Seeing him off, I noticed my hand closing the door behind him.

That afternoon, sitting in my living room and looking at the mountain he pointed out, I resolved to venture into the wood myself. What I needed was some time alone. The questions posed by my present situation became exceedingly unbearable. I was not only mournful but also broken. I had nothing left to give. Worst of all, I felt deceived. My life, my marriage, my motherhood, my career, my income, my hopes, my beliefs, and convictions were all destroyed in an onslaught of reality I was unable to fathom. Nothing was anymore the way it had seemed.

The next day, Luna and I arrived at a trailhead at the foot of the mountains for an afternoon outing. Packing some water and a sandwich we hiked into the wood and quickly found ourselves alone. The experience seemed peaceful at first but a few miles in this changed in an instant.

Walking down a wooded ravine, I heard leaves being disturbed behind me. As I turned, I noticed both the acceleration of my heartbeat and a cold, chilling sensation creeping down my neck. In the past, I had always been afraid of the forest and could venture in only peripherally before a gloomy feeling made me turn back. The objects of my fears were the lions and bears. I knew that the greatest threat in this wilderness was exposure and the resulting hypothermia. Nevertheless, it was the large predatory animals that played most vividly on my imagination. The primordial anxiety of being preyed upon seemed to override most other sensations. I had walked with Luna in this area before, and sometimes saw the carcasses of deer dangling in trees high above the ground. I knew that should I be threatened I would have to stand my ground. And as I turned and fixed my eyes on the area from which the disturbance came, the corner of my eye beheld a swift motion unexpectedly far away from the spot that had commanded my attention.

My heart seemed to miss a beat as I turned my head. And there it was. For a blink of a second I saw a lion in its entirety as it moved with dazzling speed. That blink of a second, though, seemed longer. The lion was about seven feet long and must have weighed two hundred pounds. Its fur was golden with white fluff on its belly; the tail was stretched parallel to the ground as if it were being pulled along. Its head was turned toward me as it fixed me eerily with its gaze. And just as our eyes met it disappeared behind a rolling hill.

All suddenly became quiet. I stood frozen solid, unable to move my gaze from the area were I saw the lion. It was a remarkable moment, for just as fear had turned into a heightened sense of awareness, so too, had my racing mind fallen into silence.

So there I stood. I dared not remove my eyes from the hill behind which the lion vanished, for fear it would reenter my world from the same place. Slowly, though, I realized that the cat could be anywhere, given its speed and agility. An attack could come from any direction and at any time.

I turned around and continued on my way only to find Luna waiting on me, tail wagging. Apparently she had missed the entire encounter. Walking along I repeatedly resisted the urge to turn around in order to assess the threat. It seemed silly to feel safe by simply observing that part of the wood that at this particular moment happened to be without a lion. The proper response to a threat, I thought, is an inner attitude of anticipation coupled with the willingness to fight.

Exiting the forest I paused and turned around. It was as if the lion had given me strength. Curiously, I seemed relieved of my fears. And so I took in this wondrous forest that stretched along over rolling hills and then slowly ascended as the waters of *Our Lady's Falls* freely fell some two hundred feet. High above the falls was said to be a beautiful valley, and further up still, a beckoning and mysterious trail led even higher to the majestic peak the Jesuit had shown me. As I stood in awe, I resolved firmly to climb this mountain and to spend a night on its peak in the glory of a full moon. Finally, I too would ascend *Mount Salubris*.

āraṇya, silva, the wood

After much planning, the day came at last. There I stood on my trailhead staring at the vast expanse of wilderness ahead of me and tingling with excitement. Some of it, in fact, was fear, but my mind had been set ever since I met the lion some four weeks earlier. Fear, however, would no longer stop me from venturing into the great unknown. I looked in awe at miles of dense forest stretching in front of me until the trees became so small that one could no longer see them individually. In the distance, the mountain began rising far up into the sky. Dominating the first major incline was

Our Lady's Falls, a waterfall that leaped off the mountain from high above and gracefully floated down only to disappear in the green wood below. And up on top where the water left the mountain, the lush valley expanded into the mountain that seemed untouched by the world below. *Bison Valley* was its name. Just making it out from far away I realized that all the beauty I imagined from studying the map could not do justice to its real splendor. And then again far beyond and above the valley, the mountain rose even taller, disappearing into the clouds and intimating the place of its peak by its delta shape reaching into the sky. I imagined it to be above the clouds like an island floating on them in sheer reach of the eternal blue.

Mount Salubris, there you are, I thought. Always afraid of the unknown, such as the lion, I now stood ready at last. *May the lion take me if he will. But not as a coward, for if need be I will fight. But climb this mountain I will.*

And so there I stood having hopefully thought of everything. I was covered in breathable yet waterproof material from head to toe with all polypropylene layers beneath. My shoes and gloves were filled with cutting-edge insulation to prevent frostbite should I encounter snow. Most of my gear was neatly tucked away inside my waterproof frame pack and held away from my back by the frame so as to allow no moisture to build up between the pack and my back in the form of perspiration. Dangling in the front of my right shoulder was my compass, which was my guide in the fog. Hanging in the front of my left shoulder were both a whistle and a water bottle. The whistle would allow me to not appear as prey, for prey animals don't make much noise. I had chosen a metal whistle for there are no metallic sounds in nature. I had wrapped the bill of the whistle with duct tape to prevent my lips from sticking to it in cold weather. My exterior water bottle was for casual hydration only. I kept my main supply in my pack that I planned to replenish periodically using a hand held micro-filtering pump. My provisions were mostly dehydrated and had to be prepared by adding water heated on a small propane stove.

Other essential items included an eight-bulb LED headlamp, a poly-filled sleeping bag, and a bevy. My emergency pouch included another flashlight, one meal, a candy bar, five bags of herbal and two bags of green tea, twelve water-purification tablets, a space-age aluminum blanket, one hundred feet of parachute string, and a bright-orange plastic emergency poncho. My main outerwear was all forest green so that I would blend into nature instead of standing out. I also carried a lighter and waterproof matches, isopropyl alcohol, a small handheld signal mirror, a small tarp for building a shelter, and a first-aid kit containing pain and anti-inflammatory medications and some bandages. In addition, I brought plenty of athletic tape. I found it to have many uses in the forest and it is a good blister preventative.

Finally, there was my knife. It had a seven-inch blade that was pointed and was very sharp, a hard rubber grip, and I carried it on my lower right leg. Mainly it functioned as a survival knife. But carrying it in the position that I did it also functioned as a formidable weapon should I be attacked. Pounced from the rear by the lion, I would surely go down. But once there, the knife would be close by.

Caught up in the moment, I was pulled back into reality by Luna barking. Luna was a female black Labrador mix of about sixty pounds. She is ecstatic at the thought of venturing into the wood. She knew we were going out the minute I grabbed my hiking boots that morning. Once I had the boots in hand, she no longer left my side.

"Let's go!" I said in a loud and promising voice. We made our way onto the trail, my anticipation trumped only by Luna's own.

Thus began our journey. We had hiked for less than an hour when we found ourselves alone in a dense forest on a narrow trail that seemed unending. Huge trees hovered over us like giants, allowing sunlight to enter only as standing beams and luminous pillars that seemed to take turns with the trunks of the trees in holding up the canopy above. Next to the trail ran a stream. Should the trail follow the stream it would take us to *Our Lady's Falls* where the climb into *Bison Valley* began. Once on top, we would hike through the wooded valley and ascend the peak of *Mount Salubris*. What we expected on top was a full moon night of solitude, companionship, and some reflection based on the achievement at hand.

Right around then I noticed two things. Luna and I were suddenly alone. Having left the trailhead and its immediate vicinity behind us, we now encountered no more people, no more voices, no more obvious signs of civilization, and no more reason to believe we could still turn around or feel safe, for that matter. I noticed that Luna seemed to travel twice the distance I did by constantly changing her position from in front of me to running back and behind me only to come back up and into the front. I could tell that she really loved it out here in the wood. And slowly, very slowly, I realized that I liked it as well.

Here I am doing it, I thought, as something passed between the wood and me. That something was good, wholesome, and beautiful. And that something was innately already given to Luna the moment I laid hands on my hiking boots at the end of night. She was already being cradled and consumed by it the minute we had arrived at the trailhead. That something had already been animating her every step. In fact, Luna already intimately knew that something the very moment she had come into the world.

But I had never known it, I had never apprehended it, and I had never even thought of it until now. There I stood enveloped by it, tasting it, inhaling it, and being moved by it in a curious but wondrous way. Yet at the same time I could not put my finger on it and pinpoint it. Its mystery remained and suddenly I felt at ease and at home here deep in the wood. My walking slowed as I let myself become more and more absorbed by it. Even Luna was now calm and close by as if happy that we finally came here. We walked many miles without me saying a single word.

The sun was now high and I thought it could not be much longer to the bottom of the falls. Suddenly and seemingly out of nowhere there was a howling noise close by. I swung around only to hear it again. It was loud and eerie as if to foreshadow immediate danger. The pitch of the howl was high and disturbing. It was the kind of sound that could break glass. And if that weren't enough, my fear started growing even greater as I swung my head around desperately trying to locate what seemed to be a threat. Everywhere I looked, though, I found myself staring into empty spaces as if looking for a phantom. And there it was again, but this time even closer. The sound seemed to originate within thirty feet but wherever I looked I saw nothing. Then Luna started barking nervously and uneasily. Finally, I realized that her eyes were fixed on something. Instinctively I followed her gaze into the distance.

At first I thought it was a wolf, but I realized quickly that there were not supposed to be any wolves this far south. It must be a large coyote. He was looking right at us when he suddenly cocked his head up and howled once more. Unbelievably the *prairie wolf* sounded as if he was standing next to us when in fact he was easily four hundred feet away. Suddenly, knowing that his location had been spotted, he got up and scurried from the massive rock he was sitting on and disappeared into the wood. Luna and I stood there staring. In the end, when I broke my stare and turned to Luna, she immediately reacted by hurrying to me and wagging her tail like a puppy, soliciting reassurance and a little love. Petting calmed her down, as we both seemed to agree that there was no more danger. The howling resumed, but this time from far away. Once again we strained to locate the source. I tried to calm my fear by reasoning a great distance between the terrifying noise and us. And although far away, the howling grew so aggressive and threatening that I realized there must be many of them instead of just one. I immediately glanced at Luna to see if she had located them, and I was shocked to see her growling and fletching her teeth as though an attack were imminent. Following her gaze my mouth opened in terror.

There in front of us, perhaps forty feet away, stood a huge coyote flanked by two others. Then a fourth one became visible, moving out and into the front of a tree to my right. Our lives seemed suddenly in danger and I could think of nothing to do but stare back at the aggressors in anxious anticipation of the worst. Stunningly, as two of them snarled and fletched their teeth before us, the others howled. And as they did, their eerie sounds seemed far away rather than right in front of us where they actually were. Slowly, step-by-step, they came closer. Luna poised herself in front of me so as to engage them In battle. Her movement momentarily halted their advance as they realized that there would be a fight instead of mere submission. Luna's hair spiked off her body and she growled in a way I had never heard before. Her voice was much lower and more forceful than that of the *little wolves* as she infuriated them by what seemed to be an invitation to fight. Encouraged by my dog I reached down my leg, opened the sheath, and drew my knife.

And then the most unexpected thing of all happened. Without a single conscious thought, I jolted to the right and charged the fourth coyote at full speed, screaming at the top of my lungs. The wild dog was less than thirty feet away as I closed in on him under the surge of an overwhelming and primordial determination to fight. The coyote flung his body around and fled. Arriving in his original place, I stopped and let out a yell that scared no one worse than myself. Regaining my mental composure, I swung back toward Luna to assess her fate. There she stood, alone and looking at me with her tongue hanging out and breathing fast. The coyotes were gone—all of them.

After lots of petting, Luna and I calmed down and resumed our journey. I remember feeling strong and in control of our physical well-being. This in turn brought about a sense of heightened joy and euphoria blended with sheer freedom. *We are someone too,* I thought. We were not just a walking free lunch to any carnivorous beast that happened along. Out here, I realized, I could also be a wild beast and a formidable threat to any aggressor. Understanding this gave me a sense of unequivocal presence in the wood.

We had walked only a few hundred feet further, when we suddenly heard the falls. The roar of water smashing into the bottom pools slowly drowned the temperate chatter of the brook next to our trail. The waterfall became louder and louder as we approached until its sound enveloped us completely. Luna started barking with excitement and running around me in circles as if we had just crossed a great desert and had cheated death. Then she ran up to one of the pools and began drinking her fill. I simply stood there detecting harmony in the wall of sound that surrounded me. And as my mind gradually tuned in to the experience I also noticed the mist building up on my head,

83

face, and hands. A slight breeze mingled with the mist. It felt not cold but fresh, not wet but clean, not foreign but friendly. Once again the wood welcomed me with all of its sensations, and I felt at ease. Looking up, I could see the falling water floating down as if slowed by grace itself. I was happy for the first time in years.

Just north of the falls the trail ascended the incline in a serpentine way. Slowly we hiked along, making pause every three or four hundred feet to catch our breath. My frame pack seemed to increase in weight as we gained elevation. But stopping frequently also afforded us an ever-broadening view across the plains and a distinct sense of both remoteness and altitude that was wholly absent when viewing the mountain from the bottom up. The falling water still blocked out all other sounds, though I could no longer feel the cooling mist. I was sweating profusely and laboring my way up the mountain when I became aware of the top only a few hundred feet away. Luna didn't appear to be bothered by the steep angle of our ascent as she periodically lunged off the trail in pursuit of chipmunks. Focused on the small and furry animals she would run at full speed regardless of whether she was heading down hill or up. I always wondered what she would do if she ever caught one, but she never did.

Arriving at the top, we found ourselves at the very mouth of *Bison Valley*. Down the center of it flowed the stream that flew over the ridge and descended the fall. Through the small valley, however, it trickled peacefully as flowers, insects, and butterflies kept it company. The canyon was about two miles long and a half mile wide and seemed untouched. Standing on top of *Our Lady's Falls* and looking into the canyon, I felt as though I was standing at a gateway to a different world, a portal that led us from the real to the surreal. The Jesuit's words came to mind when he described the mountain as a peculiar one. Turning around and looking east, I realized that the horizon in the far distance was no longer straight and that I could make out the curvature of our planet.

The beauty of the canyon was overwhelming. On both sides of the stream were rolling carpets of green that felt soft and moist to the step. Sprinkled onto them were small patches of color that ranged from bright yellow and soft blue all the way to ember orange and fiery red. These little groups of flowers seemed to enjoy all the space they could ever need as they danced in the wind.

As the roaring torrent finally lost itself in the background, our hearing was treated to the tranquility of the forest and the whisper of the wind as the water splashed along slowly.

What a great place to rest and refill my canteens, I thought as I took off my pack and prepared for a picnic. Luna found a patch of moss that welcomed her as she stretched her body over it and began to nap. I located my micro-filter and knelt down by the brook to start pumping. The water was ice cold. It was so clear that those parts of the stream that were not challenged by rocks and other obstructions appeared wholly transparent. The streambed was composed of fine sand that made the silt filter attached to my intake hose very useful. Every time I sucked water into the pump, sand rushed into the silt filter. Every time I pushed water through the pump, sand poured out of the filter and back into the stream.

What happened next all took place in slow motion. As I sat pumping, I heard the breaking of twigs and small branches. I looked across the stream in the direction of the sounds. I could see only trees, for the forest was quite dense. The sounds, however, came closer and suddenly I could make out a large shape. As it came closer, an unwelcome idea introduced itself to my mind. Actually, I momentarily denied the idea as if I could counteract reality. It didn't work. There, perhaps thirty feet upstream, stood a bear. The animal took little notice of me as it leaned down and drank from the stream. Then it raised its head and stared right at me. At that moment, my system simply shut down. Consumed by the stare I neither thought nor acted. From this moment on all I did was exist.

The bear, as if seeing all he could see, lifted his front paws and reared. Towering at about seven-and-a-half-feet, it now looked down at me as I sat paralyzed at the water's edge. Slowly the bear stretched its neck toward me, aiming with its nose. The nose started wiggling. First, as one nostril opened the other closed. Then the tip of the nose stretched upward and caused the upper lip to follow, exposing the teeth. Then the nose moved back and forth as if trying to satisfy an itch. I could hear air rushing inward in a sniff of tremendous power. Then the whole sequence started over again. Time stood still as I experienced eternity. Finally, the bear fell back on its front paws, turned around uninterestedly, and walked slowly away.

I sat there staring at the receding beast, mesmerized. At some point I turned around looking for Luna only to find her fast asleep on her patch of moss, completely oblivious to what had just occurred. I could not believe it. What a watchdog! It was only slowly, bit by bit, while filling the canteens that I imagined myself to have been in danger. But for some reason, the experience in and of itself did not yield this presumption. This fact seemed something of a paradox as I realized the newness of all the experiences I was having on this enchanted mountain I would never have dared to visit before.

I packed my things and woke Luna. As we moved west through the valley, the peak appeared to become more distant. The higher we got, the clearer it became that it would be a two-day ascent to the top. After hiking for another hour or so, the valley came to an end as we stood in front of an incline that had not been visible from further down. I had to make a decision. Either find an adequate place to spend the night at the foot of the incline where it was wooded or ascend a bit more in the hope of finding a place that afforded a better view, one, perhaps, that would give us some perspective of the mountain itself and the plains that stretched out before it far below. I decided to move on. Later, I was glad I did, for what happened over the next two days would change my life in a way I had never thought possible.

vípra, theologia, theology

The ascent was not as strenuous as the one up the falls, but I was nevertheless starting to feel fatigued. Luckily it wasn't long until we found an ideal spot to make camp for the night. It was a small rock formation that stretched east of the incline and allowed for a spectacular view. The great American desert below lay like a huge flat and brown blanket expanding to the east without the slightest bump. Once again I could see the curvature of our planet. The horizon was a beautiful arch that conjured up photos taken by the Apollo Eight mission that I had seen years before. The experience was immense and bled right into my becoming busy and making camp.

I finished setting up the bevy and made a fire. Then I found an appropriate tree about four hundred feet away where I hung my pack for the night, containing my provisions and the clothes I had worn while cooking. The surest way to have an unwelcome encounter with a bear is to reek of food while lying in your sleeping bag. Slowly, I came back to my immediate reality and was filled with joy and a sense of great achievement. Here I stood, far from the beaten path of the modern world. I was elated by the idea that I had conquered my fears of the great unknown and, of course, the lion.

Just then I saw a boy leisurely walking down the trail only a few hundred feet away. He was perhaps twelve years old and was slender, graceful, and had long silky straight black hair. The boy was American Indian. He carried a small bag over his shoulder. I looked up the trail expecting to see companions, but apparently the boy was alone. He radiated cheerfulness as he walked in a slow kind of skip and dance. Suddenly he saw me and waved. I returned the greeting as he broke from the path and headed toward me.

"How are you?" I asked as if addressing an adult.

He smiled peacefully and replied, "I'm doing well. How about yourself?"

I answered, "Fine, thank you."

"What a glorious day," the boy said as he walked over and stood on the rock overlooking the world below. It was a strange moment for me, as my intellect could not explain the boy in the present situation. Nevertheless, his peacefulness deeply affected me. Then he turned to me, and said, "It's been a long journey and I'd like to rest and move on at dawn. Do you mind company?"

"No," I replied, "not at all."

It had become dark and after sharing a snack next to the fire, we started talking. "I am on my way to see my great-grandfather," the boy said. "He lives out on the plains about two days from here."

"Is he a farmer?" I asked clumsily.

"No, he is a medicine man," the boy replied.

"What's the name of the town?" I inquired in a parental voice.

"Oh no, he has never lived in a town. My great-grandfather is a hermit. I see him in the summers to receive his teachings. He knows the medicinal properties of more than a thousand different plants that grow on the plains."

"I didn't know there were a thousand different plants that grow on the plains," I remarked.

The boy looked at me and cracked a smile as if to take some pity on me as the conversation paused.

"You know, further down I ran into a bear," I announced out of concern for his safety.

"Oh, don't worry. The bear knows everything," the boy replied.

"What do you mean?"

I slowly started to realize that the boy was utterly at home where I only a few hours ago had been a stranger.

"My people believe that the bear knows everything. Therefore we approach bears with great reverence and respect," the boy answered in a way that was more becoming of an educated adult.

"The bear, for example, can smell your intentions."

I nodded as I contemplated the idea.

"Doesn't that bother you?" he asked.

97

"No. Why should it bother me?" I replied.

"Well," said the boy, "I once told this to a man who became upset. He said he had been to college and that such a belief is mere superstition. He felt that I would do well to leave these backwards ways of thinking behind and join what he called the *real world*. As if one's heritage and culture were a matter of choice."

The temperature had dropped noticeably since sunset. I stood up and collected more firewood, and as I returned I put on a sweater.

"Do you come here often?" asked the boy.

"No," I answered, "it's my first time."

"So you're not from here?" he inquired.

"I am actually from here," I paused, somewhat embarrassed. I then added, "I just never ventured into the wood."

After some moments of silence I explained, "Up until now I was a city person I guess. I got in the habit of avoiding danger and just never thought of making my way into the wilderness."

There was an awkward silence.

"Why does the wild frighten you?" prodded the boy, who obviously could not be more at home out here in the wood.

"Well," I hesitated, "there are dangerous animals here."

"You mean like lions?" the boy exclaimed.

"Yes, like lions, for example."

The boy smiled as if he knew something that I didn't.

"You know," I started thinking out loud, "I went to college too. And there they taught me that predatory mammals that have a great

99

sense of smell can identify chemical markers by way of pheromones that other species excrete into the air through perspiration. These pheromones can travel long distances and can be detected by animals with an acute sense of smell. And the chemical markers present in these pheromones carry information as to the chemicals that are present in the bloodstream of the animal that secreted them in the first place. Adrenalin, for example, is found in the bloodstream of an animal that is agitated or aggressive. And a bear, I am told, does not merely have a good sense of smell but one of the best. Therefore, if a bear identifies such a chemical coming from you through the air, he knows that you are a threat and will act accordingly.

That is to say, the bear could attack you or try to flee. Likewise, should he identify fear through a chemical marker he could decide that you are either possible prey or that you are no threat, whatsoever, and disregard you while going about his way."

I realized that the last option was what actually had happened to me only hours earlier. I was unable to hide my excitement. "It's all very scientific, you see," I said with a sense of pride that led into yet another moment of unexpected and uneasy silence while the boy was thinking.

Finally, he asked, "So where's the difference?"

"What do you mean?" I asked, somewhat surprised.

"Where's the difference," the boy continued, "between all that and just saying that the bear can smell your intentions?"

The question was punishing. There I sat, staring at a young boy who was already miles ahead of me in thought and who seemed to feel sorry for me. At this very moment it became profoundly apparent that I had ventured into another world. I realized, perhaps for the first time in my life, that it was time for me to be quiet and start paying attention.

"Did you see any coyotes on your way up?" the boy asked.

"Yes," I answered hesitantly.

"Did they trick you?"

Unbelieving, I stared at the boy and stuttered "Yes" once more. The surreal part of our encounter had now moved firmly into the foreground. I felt like a stranger, not merely before the boy, but in relation to the entire mountain.

"Yes, they're good at that," the boy continued. "That's why their name is *co-yo-te.*"

"What do you mean?"

"Oh, it's a long story," the boy tried to dismiss my question.

"No," I demanded, "seriously, please continue."

"Well," the boy sighed, "my mother tells me that our people believe that once upon a time there was absolutely nothing, nothing at all. This was a time before time itself. There was no world, no people, no animals, no stars, no space, nothing. And it was here that the *Great Spirit* created himself."

"Created himself?" I wondered out loud.

"Yes," said the boy in a now calm and soothing voice, "he created himself! That's why we call him the *Great Spirit*. For he alone is creator. No one else creates, only him. At any rate, when he created himself, he found himself alone. And so he wished to create a world as well. A world, that is, full of being, just like himself, where before there had been only non-being, or nothing. The world he wanted to create was supposed to be perfect, like him, and lacking in nothing.

But after he created the world, he immediately noticed that the world was not perfect but wanting in many ways. Non-being had somehow entered into the world in the form of death, for example. It afflicted all creatures of his world that were supposed to be perfect and therefore live forever. The *Great Spirit* instantly realized that his creation had been tricked somehow, that his *truth* of being had been mixed with the *lie* of non-being. And so he looked around and found the trickster. You see, *co-yo-te*," the boy explained, "means trickster in my people's ancient language. My ancestors gave the *prairie wolves* this name. Some, however, believe it also means *liar*. The *Great Spirit* realized he had been tricked. Somehow, as he created himself in the fullness of *truth* and being, *co-yo-te* also came about, unseen and unheard, only to mix his non-being and *lies* into the *Great Spirit's* creation of the world. *Co-yo-te,* though, is only half as big and half as powerful as the *Great Spirit* and can never overcome him. He can only afflict the good creation by mixing himself into it."

The boy looked at me with great concern.

"My great-grandfather, whom few believe, says that *co-yo-te* divided the people of the earth into those who serve him and those who serve the *Great Spirit*. The ones who serve *co-yo-te* learn the art of deception and may be rewarded richly in the material order of things because of it. The ones who decide to serve the *Great Spirit,* however, dedicate their lives to the *truth* and thereby must bear many disadvantages and sufferings in the material world. The *Great Spirit,* though, once aware of the activities of *co-yo-te,* created another world that is perfect in *truth* and being and excluded *co-yo-te* from it. The *Great Spirit* could be tricked only once, you see. In this new and perfect world, however, the *Great Spirit* put everything but man so that those who serve him well in this world will have a place of eternal life. In the meantime, so says my great-grandfather, *co-yo-te* remains an active force in this world always trying to debase and destroy the good creation at every level. That means physically, emotionally, spiritually, and in the end, morally. But for the ones who serve *co-yo-te,* there will be at best nothing when their time here comes to an end. According to my great-grandfather, *co-yo-te* has tricked them into believing the *lie* that this world is all there is. Sadly, they therefore might never even know that they were tricked. My great-grandfather, though, believes strongly that the purpose of this life is to attain the next. This, however, is only possible if one denounces deception and dedicates one's life to the *truth."*

I was amazed at the boy's insight into my experience with the coyotes and their deceptive ways. Surprisingly, I found myself deeply respecting his views.

After a moment of reflection I commented, "Your great-grandfather seems to be a very wise man."

"I think so," replied the boy, "but our people are divided as to the *truth* he speaks."

Following a brief silence I remarked, "Many of my people believe that God, which is what we call the *Great Spirit,* has always been, rather than having created himself. And one day, before he created the world, he created helpers in the form of purely spiritual beings called angels. Then he created the world and put man into it. And the world at first was perfect. But then some of these angels, one-third of them to be exact, led by one in particular named Lucifer, rebelled against God and wanted to be like him. This was not possible, because they are creatures like the rest of us. They decided from then on to attack the good creation by bringing death and the *lie* into it. And the original people of this world bought into the *lie*. That's when the trouble began. The results are much the same as in your great-grandfather's story."

A small silence stretched between us.

"My people are divided too," I continued. "Some also think that this world is all there is and that morality, which is what we call the belief in the non-material meaningfulness of our decisions, is an illusion. Therefore, just like in your story, the art of deception is practiced widely for material gain. Mostly, I was like that also, although I have never felt comfortable about *lying* to get my way. Others, however, believe that there is more to it."

"And there is," interrupted the boy.

"Materially, for example," he continued, "if a person is born without a leg his body does not reflect the *true* form of a human being. That is the *lie* at work physically speaking. Yet, according to my great-grandfather, every one of us is afflicted and victimized by the *lie* in

110

one way or another. The form of a *true* human being is complete health in all dimensions. In this world, though, that is not possible, for the *lie* has mixed itself with our present world from the beginning. Every one of us is wounded physically, emotionally, spiritually, or morally, or, in some combination thereof. Actually, my great-grandfather says that *lying* is not a form of evil at all. But rather, that all evil is a form of *lying*."

At this point in the conversation I found myself deeply moved. Could it be that evil was real, I wondered? Could it really be that there was such a thing as the *truth* and that there was such a thing as the *lie?* Could this be the reason life always seemed to me a puzzle into which the pieces never quite fit? Every time I thought I knew what life was about, trouble

111

began to brew. Happiness had always been elusive and I could never conclude just why. If it wasn't one thing, it was another. At times it was money, at other times it was love. Yet once my bank account was happy and I found myself with that particular person, I began to long for something else: the job, the house, the vacation, the car, the watch, and so on. Every time I satisfied a desire, a new one popped up, like the next item on some endless list I could never catch up with.

But what the boy had told me was hard news, really a hard news. If he was right, then I *truly* never could catch up with it. For this life is either a constant struggle for material gain in competition with others, or, a struggle for meaning while constantly exposing the attacks of the *lie*. Either way, it remains a struggle.

For a moment a profound sadness enveloped me. Just as fast as it took hold, however, I identified it as mere sentimentality. It was here that I started to realize that *true* strength was the opposite of sentimentality and I began resisting it.

The boy suddenly pulled my mind back onto the mountain by destroying the silence that had captivated me.

"What took him so long?" the boy asked.

"What do you mean?" I countered, having barely regained my presence.

"Your people—they say the *Great Spirit* has always existed. He never made himself because he has existed from all eternity. Why then did he take so long to make us?"

"Because he wanted us to have a beginning," I calmly answered.

Neither of us uttered a single word for the rest of the evening; we didn't dare. Everything had been said. Any additional word could only degrade the bubble of truth we now both found ourselves in. Slowly, very slowly, we both slipped into a deep sleep as the fire became smaller and smaller until only embers remained.

Equally slowly I awoke the next morning to the songs of birds carried by a gentle breeze. As I opened my eyes, the first thing I beheld was the majestic view from what had mysteriously become *my* mountain. The plains rolled on below until the planet itself seemed to mingle with outer space. Presently I realized I was alone. I jumped up and looked around. The boy was walking away over a small hill about three hundred feet from me. Anxiously I cried out, "Hey, you!"

The boy stopped just before the hill and yelled back, "What is your name?"

"Vera," I replied as loud as I could.

"Well, Vera," the boy said, "good-bye."

"Wait," I screamed, "who are you?"

The boy smiled at me in a way I would never forget, and he shouted back just before disappearing behind the hill and from my life, "They call me *Purple Feather.*"

An hour later, I had packed my gear and was ready to move although my mind wished to linger at the place that afforded me a great view both inside and out. Feeling the rise of sentimentality, I at once turned and continued my ascent. Luna started barking as we got on our way as if to say that she wasn't ready to leave either. But it was late morning and the peak was in sight. And so we climbed. I didn't speak much that morning and Luna didn't seem to mind. The trail slowly became narrower and narrower and more difficult to navigate due to roughness and rocks that were strewn about. Nevertheless, my cheerfulness returned as the altitude increased.

In the early afternoon the incline came to an end just as the trail did and the terrain flattened and turned into a saddle about a mile long. *Mount Salubris* rose out of the saddle perhaps another thousand feet. It was a moment of great excitement for me, as visually, at least, the top of the mountain seemed within reach. Traversing the flatness of the saddle allowed my heart rate to return to normal. Trees along this flatter area were sparse, and they seemed to reach out as if to touch me. It was an eerie landscape that appeared to contain more space than necessary.

Every few hundred feet we could catch glimpses of what lay on the other side of the mountain, down the western slope. We continued on as if driven by an invisible force. Finally, we were at what seemed the last wooded area before the peak. We found the trail again and began to hike steadfastly toward our goal. After half an hour, I realized that the peak had somehow pushed itself further into the distance and that there was yet another wooded incline to ascend. Exhausted, I stopped to rest. I caught my second wind and we pushed on, but much slower than before. The altitude was becoming noticeable and I breathed deeper and faster without being able to adequately oxygenate my body. At times I even felt light-headed, but I resolved not to stop anymore. It was too painful to get started again. Luna didn't seem to mind as she joyfully ran up and down the trail much as she always did. I labored on.

Almost stumbling now, the path spiraled into the open sun and the wood gave way to the clearance of the summit. I lifted my head and saw the trail's end no more than fifty feet away. Then I noticed the ladybugs. There were thousands and thousands, perhaps even millions, of ladybugs all over the peak.

Curiously, it was only on the trail that there were few, making it possible to walk without squashing them. One could reach out to any place next to the trail and just grab a handful of them. The peak of *Mount Salubris* was thick with ladybugs.

Standing on the very top, I felt slightly dizzy as the panoramic view made its way into my mind. I slowly turned until I came full circle. It was spectacular! The breathtaking perspectives of the north, west, and south now supplemented the view to the east. To the west my eyes could wander over the great divide all the way into the snow-covered peaks of the Rocky Mountains. In the north, the foothills became greener. In the south they became flatter. The few little clouds of the day were actually below me instead of above.

I was seized with another bout of dizziness. Quickly I bent over and rested my elbows on my knees.

Luna lay in front of me, her eyes barely open, resting on what seemed to be the only patch of moss that was not covered in ladybugs. I looked at her intently and had the distinct feeling that she was not aware of the spectacular views that presented themselves. Rather, she seemed content with her immediate surroundings. I finally sat down facing east and sat there for what could have been more than an hour. I was completely at peace. There simply was not a single thought passing my mind. Finally, I had arrived.

As I gradually returned to my body, I realized that the temperature had dropped significantly. I was shivering. At once I stood up and looked around. There was no possibility of setting up camp on the peak. There was no even ground and even if there were, I would have to squash countless ladybugs making camp. But the ultimate consideration was that we were above tree line, making me the tallest object for lightning to seek out. I mounted my pack and we started the descent. I would set up camp on the flat ground of the saddle or so I thought.

Following the trail down through the wooded area just below the peak I noticed a man crossing the trail carrying wood. He briefly paused, turned toward me, and caught my eye. I thought of *Purple Feather,* who had so easily approached me the day before.

I called out, "Hello, who are you?" Realizing what I had actually said I must have blushed because it was my intention to say *how* you are and not to pry in with *who* he was.

He slowly turned toward me once again, sizing me up.

"Paul," he said. "My name is Paul."

His gaze remained fixed on me until I noticed that it was my turn to speak.

"I'm Vera," I replied.

"Well, Vera," he said, "you have a nice trip down."

The man swung around and continued walking away from the trail to the east.

Paul was large and burly, sporting a full beard, long, and mostly gray. He must have been twenty years my senior. Yet, gazing at me as he did he commanded complete attention and seemed to emanate worthiness for respect and reverence. As with most things on the upper half of this mountain, he appeared surreal, a sage-like recluse, who was on his way to an enchanted spot. I found myself taken by his presence and at once realized that just watching him disappear in the wood would surely return me to the overly simplistic and even banal world I had come from.

Summoning all my courage to fend off an emerging feeling of dread and make use of my last opportunity to speak to him, I stuttered clumsily, "Excuse me, I am actually spending the night here."

I waited for him to turn and then continued, remembering the boy's words, "Do you mind company?"

The question I uttered seemed to vanish into the huge space that surrounded the mountain as a moment of unbearable silence crept into my side of the engagement.

Then, finally, he removed what had become uncomfortable to me by calmly answering, "Actually, I don't mind. Come, follow me."

vivikta, clāritās, the clearing

And so I broke trail and followed this magnetic character into the dark shadows of the wood. We did not speak, as he never turned around during the ten-minute walk to the eastward-facing side of the mountain just below the peak. All along, Luna ran up in front of him only to turn around and run back toward me in a most joyful and playful way. It was then that I first noticed that she had never barked at him, which was highly unusual, given that he was a stranger. We arrived at a small clearing about twenty feet in diameter that was relatively flat and accommodating. I would never have found it on my own. Nevertheless, it contained beautiful patches of moss that were much to Luna's liking. In the middle of the clearing was a fireplace with a pile of wood. Paul topped it off with the wood he was carrying. There were two nice sitting-rocks next to the fireplace facing east with a view to the plains.

"Please," Paul invited me, "take a seat and feel at home." I sat down on one of the rocks and became very aware of the mysteriousness of my present situation. Had I not spent a surreal night with the Indian boy, I do not think I would have been prepared to withstand the spiritual character of this place and person. At once Paul lit a small fire, one that would not interfere with the stars above that were quickly becoming visible. There was an initial silence here as well, but it was of a different kind. It was the sort that put one at ease and allowed for the clearing of one's mind. And just as the darkness of the night came upon us, the curvature of the planet lit up in a red glow. The crest of the moon peeked over the horizon. It rose slowly, full and glorious, larger than I had ever seen it before. Thrilled, I turned to Paul only to see his face bathed in moonlight. He looked at me and smiled as If to say that my face was shining as well.

"I ran into coyotes on my way up," I spoke softly.

"Ah, yes, the coyotes," he answered.

"Do you know them?" I asked.

"Yes, I know them well. But I don't see them anymore," he replied, smiling at me.

"How is that?" I inquired.

"Well," he continued paternally, "the coyotes really hate me and try to stay away from me as much as they can. That's why I haven't seen any of them in years."

I took in what he had said and reflected on it.

Then, at the risk of being nosy, I asked, "Why do you suppose they hate you?"

Paul, still smiling at me, said, "Because I always know where they are."

Suddenly he reached down into a bag and brought out an envelope, which he casually threw into the fire. We watched it burn, briefly light up our clearing, and then crumble into ashes.

After a long pause, I asked, "Do you think there is a *truth?*"

As I uttered the question, I heard an obvious tone of skepticism in my voice. I realized that I had not fully embraced the outcome of the conversation with *Purple Feather* the night before.

Paul looked at me in his comforting way, reached down and grabbed a stick, gave it to me and said, "Sharpen this please, so that we can prepare something to eat."

Obviously he had heard my question and had chosen to ignore it for the moment, leaving me with no need to repeat it. I was left with a feeling of having hurried into the subject matter rather impatiently.

As I reached down to retrieve my knife he offered me his own knife and commanded, "Please, use this one!"

I didn't know the importance of using his knife just then but obeyed readily. As I grabbed it, I immediately felt a sense of wonder because I had never seen such a beautiful knife. It had a long sleek dark blade in differing shades of gray. The grip, shaft,

129

and tang were bright silver so as to appear almost white in contrast to the blade. The grip was made of three strands of silver twisted around each other, giving it contours, which allowed the hand to hold the knife firmly. And in so doing I realized that it was perfectly balanced.

Stroking the edge along the stick's end, he said to me, "Don't touch the blade, for it will make you bleed."

Sound advice, I thought. "You must sharpen it well."

"No," Paul answered, "actually, I never sharpen it at all. It carries its edge for life."

"How is that possible?"

"Well," he said, "it was given to me by a master blade smith who folded the metal countless times in the process of making it. That's why it carries its edge for life."

"I never knew of such a thing," I commented. "My knife is a good knife but it surely needs sharpening every now and then."

Concentrating on sharpening the stick, I decided to keep to myself for a moment or two.

Just then Paul reached back into his bag. This time he pulled out two envelopes. As he elegantly committed them to the flames, I was able to notice that the envelopes had not been opened. Finally I had to ask, "Where in the world did you get such a knife that never needs sharpening?"

Paul looked at me cheerfully and said, "I received it as I arrived in Damascus a long time ago. Well, are you done?" he asked.

"Yes," I replied, handing him the stick with my left hand and offering up his knife with my right. Taking the stick and reaching for his knife he suddenly stopped and stared at my right hand. As I followed his gaze, I saw blood steadily streaming to the ground. I dropped the knife and held up my hand in disbelief. There was a large cut across the palm of my hand. I instinctively grabbed my wrist with my opposite hand, squeezing it as if to stop the loss of blood. Crimson red, it trickled down both arms now and dripped onto the earth below.

"Relax," Paul said in a calming tone as he took my hand and wiped it clean with what appeared to be a septic cloth. I clenched my teeth to suppress the pain. Then, Paul pulled gauze seemingly out of thin air, laid it on the cut, and started bandaging it.

"What happened?" I asked in even greater disbelief than before.

"You cut yourself," he remarked casually.

"That's not possible," I said. "I am certain I never touched the blade," I added sternly.

"Didn't you?" Paul asked doubtfully.

"No, I did not!" I insisted, "I am certain. I did not touch the blade!"

Paul paused and gave me back my hand as if to say *you will be all right, kiddo*. But that was not good enough.

I was excited and became even more so as I looked at him anxiously and demanded, "Paul, what just happened?"

"Vera," he replied patiently, "you touched the blade in its full length and cut yourself. Or would you have me believe otherwise?" he added doubtfully.

I stared at my bandaged hand and stopped shaking my head and started reflecting. *No, I thought, I did not touch the blade*. My memory of handling his knife was conclusive. I had not touched the blade!

"So what do you think, Vera? Is there a *truth?*" he asked, pulling me back into the presence of our clearing illuminated by the light of the full moon.

I turned toward him, stunned at what appeared to me at the moment as a sudden change in topic.

Paul continued, "What does the evidence of reality suggest, Vera? Did you cut yourself or did you not cut yourself? Look at your hand and your blood on the ground. Could there be a *truth* about what happened or is it up to your gut feelings to decide what is actually going on here?"

Paul paused at this point as if to give me time to think. And I did.

Having reflected, I said, "I do in fact have a cut in my hand."

"Ah," said Paul, "so here is the question. Given the fact that you have a cut in your hand, must it then not follow that you have actually somehow cut yourself?"

"Yes," I conceded somewhat reluctantly, "that is what must follow."

"You see, Vera," he continued, "if there is an ultimate reality then *true* ideas must be the ones that conform to it. And the way it is given us to conform our ideas is to subject them to the evidence. Earlier you said you were certain you had not touched the blade. That was your subjective memory of the experience and your gut feeling. The evidence, however, is in your hand and what must follow from that evidence is given to you by way of reason. The point is that these things do not always agree with your opinions about them. Yet, to realize that there is a *truth* to everything, including reality as a whole, one must make the very difficult decision to go where reason takes one and stop looking for reasons that are simply meant to affirm your feelings about things."

At this point Paul's hand once again emerged from his bag as he threw another envelope into the fire. Right about now I was getting really curious about those envelopes.

Paul continued, "*Truth* is found by *seeing* and *thinking,* Vera. And one of the big problems in the world today is that modern science has become prideful due to immense technological successes over the last two centuries. Therefore, they often wrongfully believe that their method of knowing constitutes all there is to know. But their way of knowing is *seeing* only. The philosophers and theologians who do the *thinking* upon the *seeing,* however, must then complete the work. *Seeing* is merely the cut in your hand, Vera. But the *thinking* is that, given the fact that only you handled the knife, and the knife was the only sharp object you

137

did handle, it follows that the cut in your hand is there because you cut yourself. The actual cutting, though, was not part of the *seeing* but necessarily follows from the *thinking*. And do you know who these philosophers and theologians are, Vera?"

"No, I don't," I answered timidly.

"These philosophers and theologians are anybody and everybody who love the *truth* and turn their back on the *lie*. They are you and I, Vera. They are you and I! And *thinking* upon the *seeing* for the sake of *truth,* rather than *thinking* for the sake of your feelings, you will eventually reach the *truth* in your very own way. It is here that you must decide. You can acknowledge the *truth* or you can run away from it. Yet, if you acknowledge it the most beautiful thing of all happens, Vera. You will be given the gift of faith. For without faith, in and of itself, the *truth* is unbelievable. It is faith that crowns your knowledge of the *truth* and allows you to interact with it in a most personal and meaningful way."

Paul sighed as if relieved from a great burden, and then, after a short pause, added, "Learn to *see* the *lie,* Vera. And then *think* upon it. For once you know the *lie* you will know where to find the *truth.*"

Paul sat there like a sage in deep repose as I reflected long into the night on what he had said. The moon had traveled beyond our view and our small fire allowed the stars to twinkle brightly. Yet after much silence I saw Paul's hand once again slipping almost unnoticed into his bag.

Before it came back out I startled him by actually shouting, "What is it with those envelopes?"

Carefully and with great elegance his hand rose from the bag with yet another envelope, while his eyes remained fixed on me.

"These are my letters," he said in a way that made me believe he thought his utterance actually explained something.

Looking at the letter in his hand thoughtfully now, he slowly turned and offered it to me. Equally slowly I grabbed hold of it and carefully brought it into my sight, not wanting to afflict it with too much curiosity.

The letter was addressed to: *Mr. Wolf, Chaco Canyon, The Very Dead End, New*

Mexico, followed by the zip code. In the upper left-hand corner where the address of the sender goes, it simply read: *Paul, Mt. Salubris, Colorado,* followed by the zip code and the abbreviation *USA*. The first-class postage had been cancelled, implying that the letter had actually been mailed. Yet it was unopened, with a big stamp on it that declared RETURN TO SENDER.

I turned back toward Paul and asked, "You wrote these letters?"

"Yes, I did," he answered. "They are the product of a long debate I had with *Mr. Little Wolf*. True to form, though, he dropped the *Little* from his name a long time ago and has gone simply by *Wolf* ever since. We discussed the *lie* up until he realized that my love for the *truth* is complete. It was then that he stopped

141

actually reading my letters. That's how I finally realized that his hate for the *truth* is complete. And since *truth* is all I can offer, the debate ended with my last ten letters being returned to me unopened."

At this point our discussion paused. My curiosity about the contents of the letter became almost unbearable.

Finally, Paul said, "You may read them, Vera, if you want to."

"Yes, I would like that very much," I replied, experiencing some measure of relief from the painful tension of anticipation.

All at once I dug my thumb into the upper fold of the envelope and pried it open. I unfolded the contents and began reading silently.

**The greatest disservice to humanity
is to believe or promote the belief
that it is possible to lead a healthy
human life
without having an enemy.
People who believe this
are blinded by false pride
for they also subscribe to the idea
that if everyone were like them
there would be paradise on earth.**

**The enemy is the lie
and those who bear the lie.**

**The greatest lie of all
is that there is no lie.
Ultimately, this is the source
of all of man's inhumanity to man.**

**Understanding this
leads to peace on earth.**

I raised my head and stared off into the
distance where the stars gently touched the
plains. I was lost in a silence that no longer
seemed my own.

143

"Why did you come here tonight?" I heard myself asking out loud.

"To be done with my letters," Paul whispered almost inaudibly. "Please," he said gesturing to the fire.

I took both the broken envelope and the letter into one hand, reached over the fire, and let them go. Once again the paper flamed up, illuminating our small clearing only to turn into ashes and crumble away, as if into another realm. Paul and I sat there for what seemed an hour, sharing the silence that now nurtured us both.

Then, Paul rose, picked up his bag, pulled out the remaining unopened letters, and handed them to me saying, "I must go now."

He turned and started walking away.

"Paul," I asked surprised, "must you leave before dawn?"

"Yes, Vera," he replied In a peaceful way that immediately made me feel safe. "Our time together has come to an end and dawn will be a new beginning for the both of us."

I spoke as if to myself, "Will I ever see you again?"

Paul turned one last time and smiled at me, saying, "That much is certain, Vera. That much is certain."

And then he disappeared into the darkness of the wood.

This was a sad moment as I felt strongly that it would be a very long time before we would meet again. But it was different from the sadness of the night before. It seemed a source of great strength and fortitude and contained no sentimentality whatsoever. As a matter of fact, it filled me with much purpose and single-mindedness as it slowly turned into joy. There I sat, then, no longer sure as to the dream or reality of what had happened to me that night. It was as if I was waking up from a dream that appeared so real that it must have been a vision. No sooner did that thought occur to me, though, than I started remembering. I looked down into my hand and saw the small stack of letters. *Seeing* them, I knew they were real. And *thinking,* then, I knew Paul was real.

I took the top letter, opened it, and read to myself.

**Humanity differs from all other life
in that it has access to the intellect.**

**Intellect, however, ceases to be
when one and one equals three
in the same way
that one and one equals two.**

**Humanity begins by drawing a line
such that one and one equals two is true,
whereas one and one equals three is not
true.
To say it is, is a lie.**

**Befriend the lie
and loose your humanity.**

Once again I raised my eyes from the letter noticing my hand releasing it into the fire that had become smaller since Paul left. I felt somewhat alone for a moment and quickly looked around for my dear friend Luna. I found her off to my right fast asleep on a patch of moss. Reassuring myself of her company I opened the next letter, pulled it out and began reading:

147

The substances of the universe are two:
There is good and there is evil.
The good has two aspects:
The spiritual and the material.
Evil has only one aspect, the spiritual,
although it constantly tries to influence
the material world through deception.

Its essence is the lie
whereas the essence of goodness is truth.
Hence, the material world is all factual
when considered in and of itself.
Viewed in its totality, however,

the universe is but moral.

Minutes later, having committed the letter to the fire, I rose up to collect more wood. Although Paul had left me with enough wood to maintain a small fire through the night, I wished for a larger one that would allow me to read without straining my eyes. Walking into the forest immediately surrounding the clearing that had become home for the night, Luna awoke and started barking.

"Yes, Luna," I spoke softly, "I'm here."

She ran up to me and jumped up and down for joy at having found me In the dark. I collected a small pile of firewood and sat back down to watch the fire grow. Luna snuggled up against my body. My right hand gently went through her black fur. Her eyes became smaller and smaller and she dozed off again.

As I sat there I noticed that the letters struck a strange but familiar chord in me. It was as if their words echoed inside me as they sunk in ever deeper. It was as if I just came upon the taste of a particular pudding that I hadn't had since I was a child. It was as if I were recovering a memory, so to speak, that had been all but lost in the depths of my mind. Not wanting to become a victim of sentiment I pulled loose of the present moment and opened the next letter.

**Honesty is achieved when you are able
to argue with your enemies
without feeling any anger or aggression.
Hence, feeling anger or aggression
while arguing with your enemies
ought to make you aware of the fact
that you are being dishonest.**

**To have no enemy is a lie,
but remember:**

**Truth does not need the lie.
The lie, however, needs the truth,
for it is parasitic.**

Dropping the letter into the flames I immediately opened the next one.

There are two kinds of people in this world:

**The one kind divides the world into the
weak and into the strong,
and by doing so they make it self-evident
to which one of the two groups they
suppose themselves to belong.**

**The other kind divides the world into the
humble and into the self-righteous,
and by doing so they too make it
self-evident
to which one of the two groups they
suppose themselves to belong.**

**Choose well,
but remember:**

**The self-righteous are rarely strong
in the spiritual order.**

Burning the letter, I realized that by now it was impossible to ponder its contents without becoming sentimental. So I let it have its way inside my mind. It was the very break of dawn now and I no longer needed a fire in order to read. Exhaustion started setting in as I realized that I hadn't slept this last night and only little the night before. I also noticed, however, that there was only one letter left. Before reading it, though, I broke camp. I used most of my water to put out the fire. I could refill my supply at the stream further down. Luna was stretching herself as if to advertise her comfort level. Then she looked at me and yawned.

I walked about the clearing picking up and packing all our little things, making sure we would leave only footprints behind. Then I sat down one last time holding Paul's final letter in my hand, while out in the distance the crest of the sun pierced the horizon like a great spear piercing the heart of a mighty warrior. *Seeing,* I saw the sun rising. *Thinking,* though, I saw the sun rising *again,* as I opened the envelope . . .

Hope is the act of cultivating humanity.

**Cultivating humanity
is the act of falling in love with the truth.**

**Falling in love with the truth
is the act of moving away from the lie.**

**Thus, sooner or later one will escape the
reach of the lie.**

**In this new situation, though,
one ought not think oneself the better**

**for that is false pride based on the idea
that one no longer has an enemy,
which, of course,
is the lie reaching and embracing you
effortlessly.**

**Therefore, it is actually not you who is
cultivating humanity,
but the truth that is cultivating you
through humanity.**

**Here, false pride does not enter and you
may remain aware.**

**Aware, that is, of the fact that you have
an enemy!**

Lighting a match I set fire to the last letter
and held it by a corner until the flames burnt
the tips of my two fingers. Then I rose, called
Luna, and went home.

ṛtá, solvō, freedom

It has been a year now since I came down from the mountain and out of the wood. It has been a hard year. At first I didn't speak about it at all. I was fearful that small talk or casual conversation would somehow degrade the memory of those events I have come to cherish so much. My new friend, the Jesuit, knew right away, however, that the outing had changed me. He never pushed me to talk about it, though; he could sense very clearly that the moment would come. And one evening, while visiting me, it finally did. All at once, he was listening and I was speaking. I told him everything in general, but about a man named Paul, in particular. We never looked at each other as I spoke, but rather, it appeared

155

to be his very own and private experience to take the story in, as it was my very own to tell it. When I had finished, we sat in silence. He never said a word. It was the best comment he could have given.

Often now I find myself standing in the back yard and staring at the mountain of which I have grown so fond. One time, I noticed my friend's hand on my shoulder as he also looked into the distance and shared his knowledge with me that it was there that I had been told a story in the wood.

Once I even cried while gazing; but it was a good cry, one that lacked sentiment and had a life all its own. My emotions have become clearer to me as they deepen day by day.

Twice since I have ascended the mountain, but *Purple Feather* and Paul were not there. Most else was, though: the falls and the mist, the stream, the animals, and even the ladybugs on the peak. All except the clearing where I spent the night with Paul. Search as I will, it is simply not there anymore.

Fr. John no longer shares his worries about me disappearing in the forests for a week at a time now, with my dearest companion Luna. He shelters his anxieties and grants me the gift of knowing that he understands. Father knows that this is what I have to do and that this is what makes me who I am today. He knows that even if someday I should not be able to return from the wood on my own strength, he would somehow, mysteriously perhaps, find the power to forgive me.

Our friendship has grown in the past year to the point where we need fewer and fewer words to share things with each other. Our decisions to embrace the *truth,* his explicit and mine unspoken, fulfill and complete the trust we have for each other.

The evening we shared my experience with Paul, I slept like a little child. And I will never forget the next morning. I awoke feeling great, and no sooner than was I up than I went downstairs into my library, grabbed a piece of paper and a pen, and started writing my very own letter addressed to no one in particular:

**Barring only physical restraint,
freedom is always**

**and never anything other
than freedom from deception . . .**

THE END